JACK

THE STORY OF A BEAVER

SHIRLEY WOODS

ILLUSTRATED BY CELIA GODKIN

Fitzhenry & Whiteside

Text copyright © 2002 by Shirley Woods
Illustrations copyright © 2002 by Celia Godkin

First published in paperback in 2003.
Published in Canada by Fitzhenry & Whiteside, 195 Allstate Parkway, Markham,
Ontario L3R 4T8
Published in the United States by Fitzhenry & Whiteside, 121 Harvard Avenue, Suite 2,
Allston, Massachusetts 02134

www.fitzhenry.ca   godwit@fitzhenry.ca.

10 9 8 7 6 5 4 3 2 1

National Library of Canada Cataloguing in Publication Data
Woods, Shirley E
Jack : the story of a beaver / by Shirley Woods ; illustrated by Celia Godkin.
ISBN 1-55041-733-9 (bound).—ISBN 1-55041-735-5 (pbk.)
1. Beavers—Juvenile fiction. I. Title.
PS8595.O652J32 2002   jC813'.54   C2002-901606-1
PZ7

U.S. Publisher Cataloging-in-Publication Data (Library of Congress Standards)
Woods, Shirley.
Jack, the story of a beaver / by Shirley Woods ; illustrated by Celia Godkin. – 1st ed.
[96] p. : ill. (black & white illustrations) ; cm.
Summary: The world is a dangerous place for a young beaver. And Jack, along with his
siblings, learns quickly that even their den is not always safe. But the world has many
adventures, and as Jack matures, he finds, one day, that he is ready to start a family of
his own.
ISBN 1-55041-733-9
ISBN 1-55041-735-5 (pbk.)
1. Beavers – Fiction – Juvenile literature. 2. Family life – Fiction – Juvenile literature.
[1. Beavers – Fiction. 2. Family life – Fiction.] I. Godkin, Celia. II. Title.
[F] 21 2002   CIP

Fitzhenry & Whiteside acknowledges with thanks the Canada Council for the Arts, the
Government of Canada through the Book Publishing Industry Development Program
(BPIDP), and the Ontario Arts Council for their support for our publishing program.

Design by Blair Kerrigan/Glyphics

For my grandson Jack

Shirley Woods

Author's Acknowledgements
Many people have given me valuable insights into the behavior
and life of beavers. In this connection, I am especially indebted
to Bob Bancroft, Larry Nicholson, Glenwood Rhodenizer, Don
Troop, and Neil Van Ostrand.

Celia Godkin has taken a special interest in this story, and
her superb illustrations do much to enhance the book.

I also wish to express my appreciation to Ann Featherstone for
her skill and sensitivity in editing the manuscript.

Finally, I must thank my daughter Julia, not only for her
excellent advice but also for producing Jackson Bartlett Owen,
to whom this book is dedicated.

---

*With thanks to Steve Gilbert
for teaching me everything I know
about pen & ink.*

Celia Godkin

CHAPTER ONE

A BEAVER IS BORN

Hidden in the vast forest north of Lake Superior is a beaver pond. The pond is nestled in a little valley, surrounded by trees. Few humans, except for cottagers and trappers, visit this rugged country. It is home to the bear, the wolf and the porcupine.

•

Spring arrived in the valley on the fifteenth of May. By this time, pussy willows had shed their catkins, and the leaves on the alder bushes were the size of mice ears. Bright tufts of grass dotted the beaver meadow. At the edge of the pond, green sprouts showed through the faded weeds. While the pond shimmered in the sun, black flies and fragile mayflies danced over the brown water.

Perched on a reed, a red-winged blackbird

welcomed the season. *Konk-a-lee, konk-a-lee, konk-a-lee!* From the shallows, tiny tree frogs joined in the chorus. *Peep, peep, peep.*

•

That night the temperature dropped. Frost drifted down the valley, chilling the needles on the spruce trees. When the cold air settled on the pond, the surface grew still. Soon the dam and the beaver lodges sparkled with ice crystals.

The stars were fading when a sleek head popped out of the water. The beaver looked around for a few moments, then started across the pond. He swam silently, trailing a silver vee-shaped ripple in his wake. When he reached the shore, he clambered out and shook himself. Drops of water flew in all directions. Then, with considerable care, he groomed his dense brown fur.

The beaver was the father of the colony. He had a thick body with a short neck and a blunt head. From the side he looked as though his back was humped, because his hind legs were longer than his forelegs. His most unusual feature, however, was his tail. It was shaped like a paddle. And, instead of fur, it was covered with scaly, black skin.

Before leaving the safety of the water, the beaver paused to listen and to sniff the breeze. Then he waddled into the meadow to get his breakfast. It took only two bites with his sharp front teeth to cut a tall willow. Grasping the butt end in his jaws, he dragged the shrub to the pond. At the water's edge he cut the slender trunk into three manageable pieces.

Picking up a section in his forepaws, he tore off a strip of bark with his teeth. It tasted good. Deftly he rolled the stick in his paws and nibbled the bark like corn on the cob. Soon he was down to the bare wood. He dropped the stick and reached for another. When he'd finished the trunk, he ate the branches and the shiny leaves.

Then he returned to the meadow. He was no longer hungry, but he wanted to bring some food home to his mate. Retracing his steps, he cut a willow from the same clump as before. With the butt end of the willow firmly in his teeth, he turned to go back to the pond. At that moment a quavering howl rang through the forest. *Awooooo!*

The cry of a wolf.

Taken by surprise, the beaver dropped the willow. Looking around, he tried to pinpoint the sound. All he could see were the treetops against the ink-blue sky. A curtain of black shadows hid everything else. He waited and listened.

Awooooo! To his relief, the call came from the far side of the valley. The beaver relaxed. He knew he had plenty of time to get to the pond. Picking up the willow, he set off again.

Another wolf call rent the air. The beaver took a few steps, and stopped.

The last howl had come from his side of the valley. And it was much closer. At once he realized what was happening. The wolves had split up, and they were closing in on him from both sides.

There was no time to lose.

The beaver hurried along the path, towing the shrub, but the branches kept getting snagged in the grass. Reluctantly he let go of his burden. As he did so, his ears picked up a faint noise in the undergrowth — the sound of a paw breaking through ice on a nearby puddle. Thoroughly alarmed, he ran as fast as he could for the pond.

He plunged in with a splash. Propelled by his webbed hind feet, he swam underwater until he was close to the lodge in the center of the pond. When he finally surfaced, a large gray wolf was watching him from the bank. A moment later a second wolf appeared.

The beaver had nothing to fear, for the wolves could never catch him in the water. Even so, he chose to warn the other beavers in the colony. Rearing out of the water, he slapped the surface with his tail. *Whack!* Then he dove again.

By the time the ripples subsided, he was safe inside his lodge.

•

Some years earlier a pair of beavers had dammed the stream that ran through the valley. The dam, made of sticks and mud, blocked the flow of water and created a pool. As the water backed up, the stream overflowed its banks and flooded the low ground on either side. Now the pond was larger than a football field.

There were two beaver houses in the pond. Dome shaped, they looked like untidy piles of sticks. The father beaver had fled to the one in the middle of the pond. The other lodge was partly on land. It was built on the tip of a point and was surrounded on three sides by water.

Each thick-walled lodge contained a den with two levels of living space. By the main entrance hole there was a place for the beavers to dry off and to eat. Above this muddy area was a dry sleeping platform.

The dens could only be entered from under the water. This prevented land predators — like wolves and bears — from following the beavers inside. The lodges also had escape tunnels to avoid underwater enemies. If an otter swam in one entrance, the beavers could escape out the other.

•

Until recently, the father beaver had lived with his mate and their three offspring in the shore lodge. But two weeks ago the mother beaver had forced them all to leave. This was normal, for she was expecting another litter, and needed space and privacy to have her babies. Father beaver and the three yearlings moved to the lodge in the middle of the pond.

As soon as her mate left, the mother beaver cleaned out the dried weeds and bark that covered the sleeping chamber. She replaced the old bedding with a layer of soft wood shavings she had stripped with her teeth. When the natal den was in order, she made herself as comfortable as possible, and waited.

She went into labor the day her mate escaped from the wolves. Her first kit was born just after dawn. Sitting on her tail, she held the baby in her paws and licked it clean. Then she fed it with her milk. It was mid-afternoon by the time her fourth and last baby was born. His name was Jack.

Just before Jack came into the world, a white-throated sparrow lit on the roof of the lodge. The little bird was in its spring finery, with a striped cap and a bright yellow eye patch. At the moment of Jack's birth the sparrow broke into song. *Sweet sweet, Canada Canada Canada!*

Jack had one sister, Sleek, and two brothers, Slap and Chopper. He and his littermates were born with their eyes open and baby teeth. Their soft brown fur lacked the long guard hairs that protected their parents' underfur. Their tails were about the size of a man's thumb. With their bright button eyes and short woolly coats, they resembled stuffed toys.

For the first few hours Jack couldn't focus his eyes, and was hardly able to move. Mewing and squeaking with hunger, the babies stayed close to their mother. From time to time she would pick them up and feed them. As soon as they found a nipple, their squeaks

would change to smacks of contentment.

Jack's father came to the lodge at dusk that evening. He emerged from the entrance hole carrying a lily root in his mouth. He had dug the root out of the muck at the bottom of the pond as a present for his mate.

The beaver couple nuzzled each other in greeting. While Jack's mother ate the root, his father inspected the new family. The babies were asleep in a pile. Picking each kit up in turn, his father sniffed it, then gently returned it to the heap. When his curiosity was satisfied, he eased himself back into the water and disappeared. He would return, however, to help take care of his offspring.

But Jack knew nothing of this. Only one day old, his world consisted of his mother. He didn't know his father existed, having slept throughout his visit.

CHAPTER TWO

AN UNWELCOME VISITOR

It began to rain shortly after dawn. The rain dimpled the surface of the pond and beaded the lily pads. In the grassy meadow yellow coltsfoot and marsh marigolds opened their petals to the sky. At the end of the point the beaver lodge shone wetly in the morning light.

Inside the lodge it was snug and dry. Jack's mother heard the patter of rain on the roof but paid no heed. She knew the den could withstand the harshest weather. Her main concern was keeping an eye on her young family.

Jack and his littermates were ten days old. They had developed rapidly during this period. On the day they were born, they could barely crawl; now they were bounding about the den. Using their tails as props, they could even stand on their hind legs like their mother. And they had learned to use their delicate front paws like hands. Jack practiced this new skill by picking twigs and shavings off the floor.

Jack's mother still suckled him each day. But he'd also begun to eat leaves and twigs. He managed to eat solid food by cutting it into small pieces with his front teeth. After he was weaned, he would live on bark, twigs, leaves, buds, water plants, roots and grasses. When he was older, he would use these same teeth to cut branches as thick as a man's wrist and to fell trees as tall as a house.

Like all beavers, Jack's front teeth were positioned so the upper two rubbed against the lower two. The grinding action kept his long incisor teeth sharp as chisels. To offset the wear from constant use, his incisors would grow throughout his life.

The little beavers began to walk when they were three days old. Their first steps were unsteady, and they often bumped into each other. Sometimes the gentle collisions led to a wrestling match. As the kits became more sure-footed, they went on to explore every nook and cranny in their den. Then they graduated to games of tag and chase.

The mother beaver was very patient with her babies. She let them climb all over her, tweak her fur, and ride on her tail. So long as they stayed on the upper level of the den, they could do whatever they liked. But they were not allowed on the lower level where there were plunge holes. When a kit strayed too close to the edge of the sleeping chamber, she would pull the little one back.

One day, while their mother was having a nap, Jack and Sleek played a game of tag. Though Sleek was smaller than Jack, she was quick on her feet. Jack ran all over the den, but he couldn't shake Sleek off his heels. Putting on a burst of speed, he circled the den twice. This didn't work either. Then he suddenly changed direction and jumped off the sleeping platform.

He landed on the lower level and set off again. After a few steps he glanced over his shoulder to see if Sleek was behind. The next thing he knew, Jack was falling. With a plop, he landed in the entrance hole. Squealing with fright, he kicked his feet and tried to get out. Instead, he swam in circles.

The commotion woke his mother. She knew immediately what had happened. In seconds she was at his side. With a scoop of her paw she grabbed Jack's tail and fished him out of the water. Other than being wet and bedraggled, he was fine.

After a scolding, Jack's mother licked him dry. Then she waterproofed his wooly coat. Using her nails, she combed oil from the glands between her legs into his fur. Because the young beaver would spend so much time in the water, oiling was a vital part of the grooming ritual. Jack, who was just seven days old, wasn't mature enough to do this for himself.

In the next few days, all the others in the litter managed to fall or jump into the plunge holes. Chopper enjoyed the water so much that, after being dragged out, he went right back in again. The second time, his mother grabbed him by the scruff of the neck with her teeth and pushed him all the way up to the sleeping chamber.

The mother beaver wasn't worried her kits would drown — she knew they could swim. She didn't want them near the plunge holes because she feared underwater predators. Should an otter come up one of the tunnels, it could snatch a baby in the blink of an eye.

During their first week Jack's mother looked after the babies by herself. When she left the lodge at night to feed, their father would baby-sit for her. The next week, two of the yearlings returned to the natal lodge. Born the previous spring, the yearlings had come to help look after their young brothers and sister.

•

Not far from the pond a black bear pushed through the dripping bushes. He moved slowly, swinging his head from side to side. He was searching for food. When he came upon a fallen spruce, he clawed a patch of bark from the trunk, hoping to find grubs. There were none, and he shambled on.

The bear had hibernated in a cave up the valley. Through the winter he lived off the body fat he had stored the previous autumn. When he woke in late April, he still looked plump. But beneath his glossy black coat he was thin, and he had lost a lot of weight.

Early spring was a hungry time for bears in the north. There was little vegetation to eat, and most young animals were still in their natal den. For the first two weeks the bear had managed on the last of his fat reserve. Now that was gone, and he had to hunt hard each day to survive. During this difficult period he ate whatever he could find — moss, carpenter ants, beetles, fresh sprouts of grass, and even spruce needles. Anything to ease the pangs of hunger.

Pausing from time to time to check the banks of the stream, the bear worked his way down to the pond. When he came out into the open, he stopped to taste the breeze. His sensitive nose caught the faint scent of beaver. He turned his head in the direction it came from, but he was too nearsighted to see anything. Walking quietly, he followed his nose.

With each step the scent grew stronger. Then he saw the beaver lodge on the point. Stealthily the bear climbed the dome to the air hole at the top. Below he could hear the beavers murmuring to each other. Snuffling with excitement, he put his nose to the latticework of sticks and inhaled deeply. The musky aroma made him drool.

•

The mother beaver looked up in alarm when she heard the roof creak. Her two yearlings also heard the sound, and looked up. Jack and his littermates were playing and took no notice.

Above them something blocked the light that filtered through the air hole. Then a series of blows shook the lodge. This was followed by the crunch of breaking branches. The mother beaver suddenly caught a whiff of the intruder's scent. It confirmed her worst fear — a bear was trying to break in.

Jack's mother herded the kits into a corner. She was terrified. She knew they were trapped. Her little ones were too young to dive, so they couldn't escape through the plunge holes. And she couldn't leave them. If the bear broke into the den, she would defend her babies to the death.

The bear continued to swipe at the lodge. Shaking with fear, the two yearlings watched their mother for a sign. When dirt began to fall from the ceiling, she hissed at them to flee.

The yearlings shot out of the lodge like two brown torpedoes. Far out in the pond, one of them popped to the surface. Then it slapped the water and dove. The bear heard the smack, and saw the trails of bubbles leading from the den. His prey had escaped. Before giving up, the bear listened at the vent hole to make sure no beavers were left in the lodge.

•

Jack's mother didn't know why the noise above had stopped. What was the bear up to? Drawing her babies close, she hoped they wouldn't make a sound. Then she heard heavy breathing at the air hole. The seconds ticked by. After what seemed like ages, she heard the scraping sound of claws sliding down the roof. Presently, there was silence. The bear had gone.

•

Further along the shore, the bear crossed the path of a muskrat foraging in the meadow. The bear followed the muskrat's trail. The muskrat saw the bear coming but was confident it could outrun such a big, slow-moving animal. When the bear got closer, it surprised the muskrat with a sudden burst of speed.

The muskrat was the bear's first good meal in days.

CHAPTER THREE

A NEW HOME

The outside of the lodge was a mess. Powerful swipes of the bear's paws had torn deep furrows in the dome. Broken branches and logs floated in the pond and were scattered about in the grass. Had the bear continued his attack, he could have broken into the den.

The mother beaver knew this. And she was afraid that the bear would come back and try again. Her only choice was to move her babies to the lodge in the center of the pond. But this presented a problem. Her kits were only ten days old, and normally they would not leave the den for the first month. It would be a hard journey for the little ones.

Jack and the others were restless from not being allowed to run about the den. To settle them down, their mother fed them. Then, with an ear cocked for the bear's return, she let them play until they fell asleep. At dusk she slipped out of the den.

She stayed underwater until she was well out in the pond. Then she eased herself to the surface, with only the top of her head and her eyes above the water. Quietly she turned and looked back at the lodge. Then she inspected the shoreline. There was no sign of the bear.

When she returned to the den, she wasted no time. Picking Jack up in her mouth, she carried him to the plunge hole. As soon as his head went under, he swallowed a mouthful of water. Then his natural reflexes took over, closing the nostrils in his nose, and the valves in his ears. At the same time clear eyelids, like swim goggles, protected his eyes.

Holding Jack the way a dog carries a bone, his mother swam quickly through the tunnel. Seconds later, they emerged into the evening air. Keeping her baby clear of the water, she started across the pond. Suddenly there was a big swirl, and Jack's father popped up beside them. Shoulder to shoulder with his mate, he escorted them the rest of the way to the lodge.

When they surfaced in the entrance hole, the

three yearlings greeted them. Brownie, one of the yearlings, took Jack. Their mother left immediately to fetch another baby. Their father, who was waiting outside, went with her.

Jack's older sister dried and groomed him. Then, holding him to her chest, Brownie walked on her hind legs up to the living chamber. The little beaver was so exhausted from his journey that he could hardly keep his eyes open. When she put him down, he curled up in a ball and fell fast asleep.

While he slept, his mother brought Sleek, Chopper, and Slap to the den. The last to return was their father. He had stayed in the lodge on the point, guarding the kits until the last was ferried to safety.

•

When Jack woke the next morning, he was ravenously hungry. He looked around and was surprised to see the den had changed. It was bigger, and it seemed to be full of adult beavers. Squeaking with fright, he bounded from one sleeping form to the other, trying to find his mother.

His cries woke Sleek, Chopper, and Slap, who were also hungry. The noise level rose sharply in the den as they added their voices to his. When they spied their mother, they all ran to her. Soon the only sounds in the den were lip-smacking murmurs of contentment. After being fed, the little ones sprawled on the floor and went to sleep.

It was then that an old beaver emerged from the shadows. His fur was almost black, and he was bigger than their father. The old beaver limped over to the sleeping kits and sniffed each one. Jack woke at the touch of his nose. When the stranger turned to go back to his nook, Jack saw the reason for his limp. He was missing one forepaw.

•

The old beaver was Jack's great-uncle. He was known as One Paw. Born seven years ago, his litter was the first in the colony.

In the summer of his second year, he left the colony to seek a mate. He traveled some distance before finding a good place to build a dam. It was on a stream that flowed into a small lake. In August, soon after he arrived there, he met a female beaver walking along the stream bank. She too had left her colony.

The two young beavers became friends. Working side-by-side they dammed the stream. After the water backed up, they built a lodge on the edge of the pond. By now, they had become mates.

One bright September day, while the beavers slept in their den, a human visited the pond. The man walked around the shoreline and studied the lodge. He was making a plan. Later in the fall, when their pelts became valuable, he would be back. The man was a trapper.

The pond froze at the beginning of November. The cold weather didn't bother the two beavers. Their coats were thick, and it was warm inside their den. They also had plenty of food, having stored enough branches under the ice to last through the winter.

Early one morning, the female beaver left the den. Several hours went by and she didn't return. One Paw was about to go out and look for her when he heard the harsh whine of a snowmobile. The machine stopped near the lodge. He heard footsteps, the splash of water and the sound of something being dragged through the ice.

As soon as the snowmobile left, he went in search of his mate. First he swam to the food pile, then he did an underwater tour of the pond. His mate was nowhere to be seen. He wondered if she might be outside, on the dam. The only way to get there was through a patch of open water at the edge of the dam.

He swam to the opening. As he pulled himself out on the gravel ledge, he stepped on a trap. The steel jaws snapped shut on his front paw. Panic-stricken, he dove back under the ice. He was able to do this because the trap was attached to a wire. The wire was fastened to the dam by a stake and anchored to the bottom of the pond with a heavy rock.

By the time he reached the bottom, his paw was numb. He tugged repeatedly to free it. The minutes ticked by, and he began to run out of breath. He would have to surface for air. But when he tried to go back, the trap wouldn't slide up the cable. The trapper had fitted a device that locked it in place, so he would drown.

He twisted and turned, becoming even more frantic. Finally, he kicked so hard that his body spun completely around his paw. The movement was so violent that his wrist parted, and his paw was torn from his body. Trailing a plume of blood, he just managed to reach the surface. Then he lost consciousness.

He was in a terrible pain when he woke, but he was able to swim back to the lodge. Had it not been for the icy water, which slowed the flow of blood, he might have bled to death. Even so, it took painful weeks for the stump to heal.

He never saw his mate again.

At the end of that lonely winter, he returned to the pond where he was born. On the slow and dangerous journey, he learned how to manage with three legs. Although he was thin and missing a paw when he arrived home, his family recognized him and accepted him back into the colony.

He didn't find another mate, nor did he leave the pond again.

Most of the time, One Paw kept to himself, although he was content to share a den. Unlike other members of the colony, he never played with the kits. If a little one approached him for attention, he would push it away.

One Paw was gruff, but he had a gift that endeared him to the colony. He hated traps, and he had an uncanny ability to detect them. When he discovered a trap, he would disarm it by pushing sticks or a clump of weeds into the jaws. His talent, which was almost a sixth sense, had saved the lives of several members of the colony. It had also discouraged trappers from the pond.

•

The night after Jack was moved to the center of the pond, his father and One Paw left the den together. They had a job to do at the shore lodge. After inspecting the damage inflicted by the bear, they set to work. One Paw collected the floating logs and the sticks in the grass. Meanwhile, his nephew filled the gashes in the dome with armfuls of mud and weeds. Then, working as a team, they replaced all the sticks and logs torn from the covering.

Day was dawning when they finished. The shore lodge was as solid as ever, with the same shaggy outline as before. Jack's father and One Paw were halfway across the pond when One Paw grunted and turned back. He had just decided to move into the shore lodge. It would be much quieter there.

CHAPTER FOUR

OUTSIDE THE DEN

By the middle of June, the pond was rimmed with grass and tall cattails, which resembled sausages on spikes. A great blue heron stalked the shallows in search of minnows and pollywogs to spear with its long beak. Offshore, white-flowered lilies floated placidly on the brown water. In the center of the pond a brook trout broke the surface to snatch a caddis fly.

When the sun touched the tree line, the heron gave a harsh *Quoawk!* and sprang into the air. Once aloft, it took a moment to compose itself for flight. Then, with its legs trailing behind like sticks and its neck curved over its back, the bird majestically sailed away.

As the heron lifted from the pond, nine furry

heads surfaced — one after the other — by the lodge. It was the beaver family. They had assembled for an important event. The kits, now a month old, had ventured outside the den for the first time.

They would begin their survival lessons this evening. But first they must know how to handle themselves in the water. They would learn this, and all their other skills, by imitating their parents.

After swimming in circles for a minute, their mother grunted for the kits to follow her. Then she set off across the pond. The little ones, flanked by their father and the three yearlings, followed in line behind her. When the mother beaver drew close to the shore, she turned around and headed back to the lodge.

Jack thought it was a great adventure. But it was very tiring. The adults swam easily, kicking their feet in unison, with their front paws held against their chest. The kits tried to imitate them, but had to kick furiously with alternate hind feet to keep up. Steering was also a problem, as they hadn't quite learned the knack of using their tails as rudders.

On the return journey to the lodge, Jack hitched a ride from his older sister Brownie. She had been watching him and noticed that he was getting tired. Quietly she swam close enough so he could scramble onto her back. To keep from slipping off, he clung tightly to the fur on her neck with his forepaws.

The kits' first outing was brief. Aided by instinct, they quickly learned to swim on the surface. But they couldn't dive yet, as they didn't know how to control their breathing. An adult had to take each of the babies down to the entrance tunnel. Once in the tunnel they were released and left to swim up to the den.

The next evening, they learned how to dive. Again, they were paired with an adult. Brownie showed Jack how to arch out of the water with a push of his webbed hind feet, then duck his head under the surface and flip his tail. He practiced these movements until he could do them smoothly. When they returned to the lodge, all the kits were able to dive to the entrance tunnel on their own.

The third evening they practiced their combined water skills. To make them more independent, their mother wouldn't allow them to follow her. Instead, she swam some distance out, then called them to come to her. When they dove, they now had to go all the way to the bottom and pick up a stone or a piece

of weed. Jack liked to dive, and he found swimming underwater as easy as swimming on the surface.

At the end of the evening the kits, supervised by their mother and Brownie, were allowed to play near the lodge. Showing off their new skills, they frolicked under the water, looped the loop, and played chase. One of their favorite tricks was to swim under an unsuspecting littermate, then rocket to the surface with a tremendous splash.

•

Now that the kits could swim and dive, it was time for them to learn how to handle themselves on land. On shore there was one golden rule they must obey. If they heard a tail slap, they were to run for the water and return to the lodge. The next night they visited the shore. All the beavers in the colony came along except One Paw. He was content to watch from his lodge on the point.

When they reached the shore, Jack's mother led her babies through the tangled weeds to the dry land. They followed in single file, so closely that they nearly stepped on her tail. After the smooth floor of the den, the thick grass and uneven ground frightened them.

For safety, their mother kept them near the water's edge. As they walked along the bank, she would stop from time to time to eat something — a flower, a fern or the root of a sedge. The kits watched her, then sampled it for themselves. In this way they learned what plants to eat and where to find them.

They went along the shoreline as far as the point. When they turned to go back, Jack caught a glimpse of One Paw in the pond. The old beaver was treading water, keeping an eye on them.

The long walk tired the little ones. Jack, who was right behind his mother, scrabbled onto her flat tail. It was like riding on a toboggan. Then Sleek jumped on too. Further along the path their mother shook them off with a flip of her tail, so she could give Chopper and Slap a lift for the rest of the way.

The little beavers were exhausted by the time they got home. However, a good sleep and some food restored their energy. Gradually they were being weaned from their mother's milk to solid food. Now she would often push them away when they whined to be nursed. But they never went hungry, for there were always leaves and branches to nibble in the den.

The kits were much more confident on their next

visit to dry land. Instead of staying in line, Jack and Chopper bounded ahead of the others. Their mother had to run and catch them. By the time she'd herded them back, the other two had also strayed. While their mother was fetching them, Jack and Chopper continued along the bank. Presently they came to a beaver trail that led inland. The two youngsters decided to follow it.

•

An hour earlier, a catlike animal had padded silently along the same trail. More than twice the size of a domestic cat, its fur was buff gray with black spots. It had a short tail, long thick legs, and large feet. Around its face was a ruff of dark fur, and its ears were tipped with black tassels. The animal was a bobcat.

When it heard the beaver kits murmuring by the pond, the bobcat left the path and slipped into a clump of alders. Knowing it must wait, it lay down and made itself comfortable. While it licked its paws and flexed its claws, it listened intently. Every few minutes it lifted its head to sweep the undergrowth with yellow eyes.

The bobcat wasn't prepared to ambush a full-grown beaver. The risk was too great, and could cost the bobcat its life. But a baby beaver was a different matter. The bobcat could kill a beaver kit as easily as a rabbit.

•

One Paw was munching a lily pad in the shallows when his nose picked up a faint odor. He stopped chewing, and inhaled again. It was the smell of a bobcat, and it came from the same direction as the young beaver family. Dropping the lily pad, he hobbled along the bank to warn them.

On the way, he passed a trail that ran inland from the water. Something told him to go back and check the trail. He caught a glimpse of a baby beaver, just before it disappeared around a bend. One Paw ran after it.

•

The two beaver kits stayed together until Jack stopped to eat some ferns. Chopper didn't wait for him but continued on. When Jack looked up, he saw that his brother was gone. Just as he started after Chopper, Jack was struck from behind and knocked to the ground. A huge beaver, hissing angrily, towered over him. It was his great-uncle One Paw.

•

Chopper arrived at the alder patch moments before this encounter. The bobcat was lying in wait for him. When the little beaver drew abreast, the bobcat pounced from the shadows. Chopper gave a squeak of terror. It was all over in a few seconds. Holding the kit's limp body in his jaws, the bobcat vanished into the forest.

•

After he'd scolded Jack and sent him back to his mother, One Paw wondered if Jack had been alone. Sniffing further along the path, he realized that two kits had strayed. The old beaver hurried along the trail, hoping to catch up with the second one.

When he reached the alders he saw it was too late. A few drops of blood on the grass and a wisp of baby fur told the story.

CHAPTER FIVE

THE STORM

Not a drop of rain fell during the last week of June. Combined with the heat, the lack of rain slowed the stream that fed the pond. The water level of the pond dropped, leaving bands of dried algae at the base of the dam and the beaver lodges. As the water grew warmer, the trout were forced to seek the cooler depths.

Despite the heat, the pond hummed with activity. Dragonflies with long iridescent bodies darted among swarms of mosquitoes, gnats, and midges. Below them, water striders skated on the glassy surface, while black whirligig beetles rowed to and fro in the surface film.

•

When Jack emerged from the den, nighthawks were swooping over the pond. He couldn't see them

against the night sky, but he could hear their liquid
Peent! calls, and the booming sound of their wings as
they pulled out of a dive. They were feasting on
insects.

Jack looked around. For an instant the pinpoint
glow of a firefly lit the velvet shadows on the bank.
Shifting his gaze, he saw his brother Slap swimming
with one of the yearlings. The yearling was towing a
heavy aspen branch. Slap followed in his wake,
carrying a twig in his mouth. In the distance, their
father was making his nightly inspection of the dam.

Now six weeks old, the three kits could come and
go as they wished. However, they rarely went out
alone. When a youngster left the den, an adult would
usually go with them. On this particular night
Brownie accompanied Jack.

Together, they swam to the shore. Ambling in and
out of the water, they nibbled the greenery along the
bank. Water lilies were everywhere. The cup-shaped
flowers, shiny flat leaves, and tender roots of the lilies
were an important part of the beavers' summer diet.

Jack ate the flowers by plucking their white petals
one at a time. The roots were also easy for him, as
they were slender enough to grasp in his paws. But

the large, heart-shaped leaves presented a problem. Brownie would deftly roll a lily pad into a tube with her forepaws, then munch the end like a carrot. When he tried to do the same, Jack's little fingers couldn't control the rubbery leaves. The leaves kept springing open, and sometimes covered his face. The only way he could eat a lily pad was to hold it flat and nibble around the edges.

After they'd eaten their fill, the little beaver decided to explore. Jack thought he'd visit the aspen grove, where he'd seen his father cutting trees. But he only took a few steps before Brownie called him. Jack pretended not to hear, and continued on. In a flash, his big sister bounded ahead and blocked his path. Ignoring his squeals of protest, she pushed him firmly back to the water's edge. It was time to go home.

The pond was wreathed in mist when they swam back to the lodge. The rest of the family returned to the den before dawn. While they slept, the rising sun painted the low clouds angry shades of red — a sign of bad weather to come.

Jack woke early that afternoon. The rest of his family was also awake. He went to his mother, hoping to be fed, but she pushed him roughly away.

None of the older beavers would play with him. They seemed grumpy and restless. He sensed something was wrong, but he didn't know what it could be.

•

One Paw sat on top of his lodge, contemplating the weather. Although it was still early evening, the cloud-filled sky was growing dark. The wind had also shifted. Normally the wind was from the west, but now it was coming from the east. One Paw sensed a storm was brewing. Far to the south he heard the low rumble of thunder. A minute later sheet lightning shimmered in the distance.

The first drops of rain splattered noisily on the roof of the lodge, leaving dark stains on the dry wood. Inside, the sound acted as a signal to the restless beavers. One after the other, they left the den.

Wind squalls riffled the surface of the pond. Then the rain began in earnest. It didn't bother the kits. They had never been out in a storm, and the prospect excited them. While the older beavers went ashore to gather food, the little ones frolicked by the lodge.

Their play stopped abruptly at the first crash of thunder. It was followed by a blinding flash that lit the entire valley. Jack was stunned. The next thunderclap was so loud it made his ears ring. At the same instant, a bolt of lightning seared through the darkness and struck a tree at the edge of the pond. The storm was all around them. Terrified, the kits dove for their den.

They only paused a moment by the entrance hole to let the water drain from their coats. Then the three of them ran up to the sleeping platform. To the kits' dismay, no one was there. Above the drumming of the rain on the roof, they could still hear peals of thunder. From time to time, slivers of bright light flashed through the vent hole. Thoroughly miserable, the little ones huddled together in a damp pile

The others didn't stay out long that night. When the mother beaver returned, she and Brownie groomed the three babies. Then she nursed each one. Well fed and surrounded by their family, the kits soon fell asleep. Meanwhile, the storm continued to swirl around the valley. Finally, around midnight, it moved away.

•

In the space of a few hours, the storm dumped a huge amount of rain on the valley. At first the thirsty land absorbed the downpour. When the ground could hold no more, the rain seeped down the

hillsides into the stream. The stream quickly
overflowed its banks and became a rushing torrent.
At the foot of the valley, the stream funneled the
water into the beaver pond.

•

When Jack's father came out of the den, it was much
cooler, and the wind had swung around to the north.
He had expected the temperature to drop and the
wind to change. What worried him were the level of
the pond and the state of the dam. The more water
in the pond, the greater the pressure against the dam.
If the dam gave way, the whole pond could wash out.

The dam stretched in an arc from one bank to the
other. It was built of logs, sticks and mud, and
anchored to the bottom by boulders in the
streambed. Over the years as the pond increased in
size, the dam had been reinforced and lengthened.
Now it was as tall as a man and as wide at the base as
a city sidewalk.

The beaver saw at a glance that the lodge on the
point was no longer connected to the land but was
surrounded by water. On both sides of the pond the
water had flooded back into the meadow. These were
bad signs. The father beaver dove in to check the dam.

As he feared, the dam had given way in several places. The worst breach was near the center. The hole must be repaired quickly, or it would widen. If this happened, the gap would be too large to mend and all would be lost. It was too big a job to do alone, so he swam back to get the others.

Everyone, except the kits, worked to repair the dam. One Paw wasn't able to carry stones or armfuls of mud, but he did perform a valuable service. He wedged himself in the main gap. While he blocked the flow of water with his body, the other beavers inserted sticks and stones behind him to patch the hole.

•

During the dam emergency, the kits were left on their own. Their mother warned them with a growl to stay by the lodge. After an hour or so, curiosity got the better of Jack. By now, the older beavers were repairing another break at the far end of the dam. With only his nose showing, Jack swam over to have a look at the repairs made to the middle of the dam. From a distance, there wasn't much to see. He paddled closer for a better look.

Suddenly, the spot he was looking at began to

crumble. Then a chunk of the wall broke loose. As the water rushed out, he was seized by the current and dragged through the opening.

One Paw, who was at the far end of the dam, saw what had happened and swam to the break. When he got there, the pond was pouring into the stream below. Far downstream, he saw a ball of brown fur. Then it disappeared below the surface. One Paw plunged into the torrent.

CHAPTER SIX

AUTUMN

Jack was powerless in the grip of the current. Bobbing about like a cork, he swirled toward the lake. One moment he was on top of the water, the next moment he was pulled under. Rocks loomed ahead, then swept by in a flash. After what seemed like hours, he was washed ashore at a bend in the stream.

He had survived the wild ride. Tiny air bubbles trapped in his fur had kept him afloat. The instant his head went under, his reflexes had closed his mouth and nostrils. But most important, though only six weeks old, he had been able to stay submerged for minutes at a time.

Bruised and bedraggled, Jack knew he must get back to the pond. In the distance he could see the rim of the dam. Swimming upstream was out of the question. The only way home was along the bank.

•

Jack hadn't walked far when he suddenly felt that he was being followed. He looked back. The trail was empty, although he thought he saw a flicker of movement behind a bush. He watched the spot, and when nothing appeared, he continued on. The sense that he was being followed grew stronger. Once again he turned around.

This time, his eyes met the unblinking gaze of a bobcat.

It was so close that it could easily have caught him. The bobcat, however, had chosen to play with its victim the way a cat might play with a mouse. For this reason, it had allowed Jack to run away. When the little beaver was nearly out of sight, the bobcat had bounded after him.

Just as it was about to pounce, One Paw charged between them. The bobcat stopped in its tracks. Twitching its stubby tail, it bared its fangs and hissed at the adult beaver. Although he was missing a paw, the old beaver was big, with dangerous incisor teeth. And he was ready to fight. For a few long moments

the attacker and the defender glared at each other. Finally, growling in its throat, the bobcat turned away and stalked into the bush.

For little Jack and his great uncle, it was a tiring walk home.

•

After the storm, the beaver colony worked all night and through the day, repairing the dam. Normally they wouldn't have been active in the daylight, but this was an emergency.

On the second night, the mother beaver returned to the lodge with her kits. Once they were safely in the den, she left them and went back to work. Jack, exhausted from his recent ordeal, instantly fell asleep. Sleek nibbled on a branch for a few minutes, and then she too dozed off. Slap paced about the den, still full of energy.

The pink light of dawn had just touched the branches covering the vent hole when Slap swam out of the tunnel. He wasn't going to play in the pond, for he knew his mother would see him. The last time he'd disobeyed her, she'd punished him with a nip on his flank. This time, he planned to sit on the lodge and watch the sun come up.

•

At the head of the valley, a female goshawk set out for her morning hunt. She left four hungry fledglings in their nest of sticks high in a pine tree. The goshawk was larger than a crow, with short, round wings and a long, barred tail. Her upper feathers were dark blue-gray and her underparts were stippled pale gray.

Alternately flapping her wings and gliding, she cruised down the valley to a favorite lookout perch. From the top of this tree, she scanned the forest floor. Presently, a red squirrel revealed its presence with a rattling *Chk! chk! chk! chk!* Turning her dark head, she spotted the twitch of its tail. Before the squirrel could finish its call, the goshawk burst through the branches and seized it.

Holding the squirrel in her yellow talons, she tore the flesh from it with her curved beak. The squirrel wasn't much of a meal, but it took the edge off her hunger. Now she must find something bigger — a snowshoe hare or a muskrat — to feed her chicks. The goshawk continued down the valley.

As she approached the beaver pond she dropped below the tree line and weaved through the evergreens. At the edge of the meadow, she slipped into a tall spruce tree. From here she could view the surroundings with the sun at her back. She had selected the perch deliberately, so her prey wouldn't see her.

Hidden in the shadows, the goshawk's red eyes swept the meadow and the shoreline. Nothing stirred. At the far end of the pond, she saw the beavers working on the dam. She glanced at the beaver lodge. Amid the jumble of sticks and logs that covered the lodge, she spied a different shade of brown. Using her binocular vision, she brought the object into sharp focus. It was a beaver kit.

The goshawk launched herself from the branch. Gaining speed with rapid wing beats, she emerged from the shadows like a thunderbolt. Just before she struck the little beaver, she thrust out her sharp claws. On impact, her talons closed, piercing the kit's chest.

•

The young beaver's squeal alerted the others on the dam. The attack was so sudden, and so swift, they couldn't have saved him. By the time they looked around, the goshawk was flying up the valley with the kit's body in her claws.

The mother beaver had now lost half her litter. In the wild, this was not unusual. But from then on she rarely let Jack and Sleek out of her sight. For the rest of the beaver colony, life continued as before.

•

By the beginning of September the nights were cool, and heavy dew covered the lodges each morning. Most of the plants in the pond had gone to seed. At the edge of the pond, brown cattail heads were beginning to unravel like beige cotton candy. Although some wildflowers — pink sundew, violet-blue selfheal and creamy ladies tresses — still bloomed in the beaver meadow, summer was drawing to a close.

As the days passed there were more signs of autumn. The rushes in the pond grew brittle, and faded from green to tan. Below the surface the bellies of the spawning brook trout turned bright orange. In the meadow the aspen leaves began to yellow, and the swamp maples flamed scarlet.

By the end of September, the nighthawks and other insect-eating birds had gone south. Most of the migrants passed over the pond, although a noisy flock of blackbirds dropped in for a visit, covering the reeds. The first of the resident ducks to migrate were the blue-winged teal. Their small cousins, the green-winged teal, were the last ones to leave.

•

One night early in October, ice formed at the edges of the pond. The first hard frost reminded the beavers of the changing season. The most urgent task was to store food for the winter. While Jack's father and one of the yearlings felled aspens and willows, the others dragged the branches into the pond. The cache, or storage pile, was located close to the lodge so that it could be reached easily under the ice.

The cache was built by pushing the butt ends of branches into the mud. As more branches were added, the pile developed into a loose mass of sticks. Eventually, the raft sunk to the bottom of its own weight.

Jack found that towing branches across the pond was difficult. It wasn't that water got into his throat. Like all beavers, he had loose folds of skin in his cheeks that he could suck behind his incisors to keep the water out. His problem was that large branches acted like a rudder and pulled him off course.

Diving with a branch in his mouth also proved difficult. Often he had to make two or three attempts before he succeeded in reaching the bottom. At five months of age he could only handle small branches.

When the cache was completed, the lodge was plastered with more mud. After watching the others, Jack and Sleek filled their paws with mud scooped from the bottom. Then, holding the mud to their chests, they swam to the surface. At first they found it hard to climb onto the lodge with their burdens, but they soon got the hang of it. Spreading the mud on the roof with their forepaws was easy.

•

On the fifteenth of October, an autumn gale swept the last leaves from the trees. The next morning, a sheet of ice, thick as a windowpane, covered the pond. At the upper end where the stream flowed in, there was a small patch of open water.

A great blue heron stood like a statue in the icy water. After an hour, it still hadn't seen a minnow. The heron surveyed the drab landscape. A chilly gust ruffled the long feathers on its back. Winter was on the way. The big bird lifted himself from the pond, circled it once, uttered a farewell *Quoawk!* and headed south.

CHAPTER SEVEN

WINTER

It was a few days before Christmas. A thick mantle of snow covered the pond, softening the outline of the lodges. Stripped of their leaves, the alders, aspens, and willows stood like gray skeletons in the meadow. On the hillsides the evergreens looked black in the cold morning light.

Nothing moved in the silent landscape. Tracks in the snow, however, revealed activity during the night. A red fox's dainty prints meandered through the meadow. By a clump of willows, the prints became widely spaced when the fox broke into a run. The fox's tracks joined those of a fleeing snowshoe hare, then both sets disappeared into the woods.

Nearby, a vole's tiny footprints ended at the edge of a cavity in the snow. A scarlet stain and the outline of wingtips on each side of the crater showed what had happened. While the vole was travelling on top of the snow, a great-horned owl had swooped out of the darkness and snatched it.

•

Despite the bone-chilling cold, a wisp of vapor rose from the vent hole of the lodge in the center of the pond. The warm air was caused by the body heat of the beaver family. Snug inside their den, each had a layer of fat and a heavy fur coat to keep them warm. When it got especially cold, they crowded together for additional warmth. Even the layer of snow on the lodge helped to keep them warm, for it acted as an insulating blanket.

Jack and Sleek, along with their yearling sister Brownie, had been confined to the lodge with their parents since the freeze-up. One Paw and the other two yearlings were in the lodge on the point. After the frantic activity to get ready for winter, the pace of their life had slowed. With the food cache just outside the door, little effort was needed to feed themselves. The rest of the time they slept or groomed their fur.

No longer a baby, Jack looked like a small copy of

his father. During the autumn he'd grown a coat the same as an adult beaver, with shiny chestnut guard hairs and short silky underfur.

By now Jack was old enough to groom himself. To do this, he sat on his haunches with his tail sticking in front of him. The most important part of his grooming ritual was waterproofing his fur. In the winter his life depended upon staying dry. If he became soaked to the skin, he could freeze to death. To waterproof his coat, he used oil from his body.

Before he applied the oil, he cleaned his fur with his forepaws and large hind feet. He was well equipped for the job, as his paws had five fingers, and his feet had five toes. He also had two split toenails on each hind foot. Jack found his split toenails especially useful for removing tangles and bugs from his fur.

When his coat was clean, he would reach between his legs with a forepaw to get oil from the glands near the base of his tail. Using his forepaws, he would then spread the oil through his long guard hairs. After this was done, he would comb his fur until it gleamed.

•

Jack's coat became very dense during the coldest part of the winter. At that time his fur was "prime" and his pelt was worth the most money. Trappers knew this, and set their traps between Christmas and Valentine's Day.

•

For Jack the day began the same as most days, with the family resting in the den. Soon after dawn a raven flew over the pond. The hoarse croak of the huge black bird echoed in the den. Later in the morning a chickadee, one of the tiniest winter residents, lit near the vent hole. With its black-capped head cocked to one side, the bird listened to the beavers murmuring inside the den. After a moment or two, it responded with a cheerful *Chick-adee-dee-dee-dee!*

The sun was high when the next sound came through the vent hole. It was the high-pitched whine of a snowmobile. The beavers stopped grooming each other as the noise grew louder. The machine halted at the edge of the pond. There was a clang of metal followed by the squeak of boots in the snow. A human was coming toward the lodge!

•

The man wore heavy trousers, a parka, and a bright orange toque. Near the lodge, he knelt and brushed away the snow with his mitt. After doing this several times, he uncovered some branches poking through the ice. Having located the food cache, he picked up his gear and moved a few steps closer to the lodge.

Here he drilled two holes through the ice with an auger, a tool that resembled a giant corkscrew. Then he joined the holes by chipping out the ice between them with a steel-bladed ice chisel. Lying side-by-side on the snow were two long spruce poles. A square trap made of heavy wire was suspended between the poles.

The trap was designed to close on the beaver's neck, killing it or holding it fast until the beaver drowned. The trap was baited with a piece of poplar branch wired to the trigger. Carefully the man lowered the trap through the hole and pushed the spruce poles into the mud bottom. The trap was now in position, between the lodge and the cache. A hungry beaver leaving the lodge could not fail to see it.

The trapper drove to the upper end of the pond where the stream came in, and set up another trap. This time, through the ice he lowered a single pole with three wire loops attached to it. These wire hoops, or snares, were large enough for a beaver's head to enter, but not so big the animal could swim through it to escape. A piece of poplar was nailed to the pole at the base of each snare. When a beaver touched the edge of the snare, the wire tightened about its neck. A locking device prevented the wire from loosening. The beaver was either strangled, or held under until it drowned.

•

Jack and the others heard the ice creak by the lodge. Then came the noise of the auger biting through the ice, and the sharp crack of the chisel. It was so close they could feel the vibrations on the floor of the den. After a few minutes of silence, they heard the trap scrape against the ice as it was lowered to the bottom.

The beavers in the lodge on the point were also listening. The yearlings were puzzled and frightened by the human intrusion. But One Paw knew exactly what was going on. As soon as the sound of the snowmobile died away, the old beaver left the den. There was no time to lose.

One Paw swam to the lodge in the center of the pond. After a brief stop to grunt a warning to the others, he went to look for the trap. It wasn't hard to find. In the milky light that filtered through the ice, he quickly spotted its sinister outline between the two poles.

The old beaver swam over to the cache and tugged a branch from the pile. Holding it in his teeth and guiding it with his good paw, he pushed the end of the branch into the trap. The iron jaws snapped shut on the branch. Now the trap was harmless. One Paw checked around the lodge to make sure there were no more traps. Then he made the long swim under the ice to the inlet.

When One Paw arrived, the two yearlings were already circling the baited snares. After he shooed them away, he scoured the muddy bottom for the right-sized stick. The snares were hard to deal with because they didn't have a spring-loaded trigger. But he managed to disarm them by pushing his stick against the inside rim until the loop became so small, that nothing could be caught in it.

•

The trapper returned three days later. By this time the hole he'd made near the lodge was frozen, and he had to cut through the ice again. When he found the branch in the trap, he thought it might be an accident. But he changed his mind when he pulled his snares at the end of the pond and saw that all three had been sprung. Stubbornly, he reset the traps.

On his next visit, the same thing happened. All his traps had been sprung. The man was about to set them once more, when he remembered what an old trapper had told him about this pond.

"You'll never get a beaver there. The place is jinxed!"

The young man considered the seasoned trapper's words, and thought, The old geezer is probably right. No sense wasting any more time.

Loading all his gear, he drove off in his snowmobile. The beavers were left undisturbed for the rest of the winter.

CHAPTER EIGHT

THE YEARLING

It was the end of March. High above the trees a pair of ravens played in the wind, tumbling, diving, and performing half somersaults. Their bell-like calls — so different from their usual croaks — rang through the valley.

Below, the evergreens were alive with smaller birds. Brown-streaked pine siskins, purple finches, and redpolls with bright ruby caps were busily eating seeds in the branches. Nuthatches hopped headfirst down the trunks, probing for insects, while woodpeckers hitched their way up the trunks, drilling for grubs and beetles. With a flash of white wings, a flock of snow buntings swirled over the meadow, then scattered like snowflakes to land among the weeds.

As the days grew longer, the warmth of the sun

freed the stream and softened the ice in the pond. By the second week of April, the dam and both lodges were rimmed with strips of open water. The ice that remained in the pond was no longer hard and clear but soft and gray.

•

Jack woke to the steady patter of rain. The first thing he noticed was a half-forgotten but welcome odor. Rising on his haunches, he sniffed at the vent hole in the roof. The scent of fresh water filled his nostrils. His excited murmurs and whistles woke the rest of the family. In quick succession, they all left the den.

When the beavers emerged, they saw to their delight the ice had gone. It was open water from bank to bank. Celebrating the end of winter, the family romped around the pond, jumping over each other, diving, and playing tag. Even old One Paw, from his lodge on the point, joined in the merriment. Swimming in dignified circles, he would pause every few minutes to give the surface a terrific whack with his tail.

After they had frolicked in the pond for an hour, the beavers swam ashore to feed. They were eager to taste freshly cut willow and poplar. Throughout the winter the family had relied on their sunken food pile.

During the past few months, however, the poplar branches had become slimy from being submerged so long, and the bark had acquired a bitter taste.

•

Jack was now a year old, and roughly the size of a cocker spaniel. As a yearling he would do his share of chores in the colony. And he would learn the survival skills of an adult. The day the pond opened, his father took him to the dam for his first lesson.

During the winter, shifting ice had eaten away at the dam, and it needed repair. So did the spillways. The previous autumn the beavers had cut several openings or spillways in the dam to prevent flooding beneath the ice. With the pond about to rise from the spring run-off of melting snow, the spillways would again be needed to relieve pressure on the dam.

Jack watched while his father expertly placed sticks, logs, and mud in the right spots to strengthen the dam. It looked easy until he tried to do it himself. At first he wasn't sure where to place the materials. Then, after his father showed him, Jack found it very difficult to insert the sticks and roll the logs so they ended up in the right position. Time and practice would solve both these problems.

•

Soon after the ice melted, Jack's mother began to act strangely. She no longer wanted the other members of her family in the den. One day, instead of returning to their den, the father beaver took his two young ones and his daughter Brownie to the lodge on the point. One Paw was now the only one living in the lodge as Brownie's two adult brothers had left the colony.

His parents' odd behavior and the disappearance of his two older brothers confused Jack. He was too young to know that these comings and goings were normal in a beaver colony. His mother didn't want anyone in her den because she was about to have another litter of babies. His older brothers were gone because they were now two years old, the age for them to leave the colony and find homes of their own.

Nor did he know that leaving the colony was the most dangerous period in a beaver's life. Wolves killed one of his older brothers. The other brother was crossing a bush road when he was run over by a truck hauling pulpwood. Brownie, who would leave later that summer, would be the only one of Jack's siblings to survive. She would meet a beaver from another colony and become his mate.

•

Jack's mother had her litter of three babies in May. Shortly after the kits were born, Sleek and her father moved back to the lodge in the center of the pond to help look after them. Jack continued to live in the lodge on the point. Although One Paw was sometimes grumpy, Jack and his great-uncle had a special bond, and they enjoyed sharing the den.

Jack had a busy summer. While the kits were confined to the den, he often visited his mother. He usually brought her food, and he sometimes baby-sat so that his mother could go out. From the end of June, when the kits ventured out of the den, Jack spent a lot of time keeping an eye on them. He also worked with his father and learned many skills, including how to fell a tree.

His father chose a poplar tree for the first lesson. Standing on his hind legs, braced by his tail, he grasped the trunk with both forepaws and turned his head sideways to the trunk. Then he bit into the tree. Raising his head, he took another bite higher up the trunk. With his long incisors, he pried out the wood between the two cuts. More bites widened and deepened the cut.

When Jack's father was part way through the trunk, he moved to the other side of the tree. Before making a fresh cut, he paused to sniff the air and listen for predators. As he chewed around the trunk, the tree began to creak and lean in one direction. Jack's father looked up, grunted to his son to follow, and dashed for the pond. Both were well clear of the poplar when it crashed to the ground. The stump looked like a pencil stub — a sure sign that a beaver felled the tree.

Jack learned tree cutting quickly, and soon became good at it. However, during the summer few poplars or aspens were cut for food. While some alders were cut to repair the dam and the lodges, they weren't eaten. There was no need. From May until September a huge variety of plants and berries were readily available around the pond.

•

Now it was October, and the needles of the tamarack trees had turned a golden color, setting them apart from the rest of the forest. Soon their needles would fall, leaving the branches bare for the winter.

•

Late one afternoon, Jack and his father were felling trees for the food cache. One Paw was helping them

drag the cuttings to a nearby canal, which the beavers
had dug to move the logs and branches more easily to
the pond.

Jack had made deep cuts on both sides of a tall
poplar, and he could feel the tree beginning to move.
But it wasn't ready to fall. After checking for
predators, he began a fresh cut. A piece of the bark
got stuck in his teeth, and he turned away to pry it
loose with his fingers. As he turned, a gust of wind
struck the tree.

It took a few seconds to realize the tree was
falling. Jack managed to turn and scramble some
distance away. But it wasn't far enough. The tree
smashed him to the ground. The force of the blow
knocked him unconscious.

When Jack awoke, the sun had slipped below the
horizon. His head ached and he couldn't move. He
was trapped under the canopy of branches. Far up the
valley he heard a drawn out howl, *Awooooo!* The
wolves were gathering for their nightly hunt. Jack
squealed for help.

After what seemed like hours, his father appeared.
The older beaver looked the tree over, grabbed a
branch, and began cutting. When he pulled the limb

away, he saw that Jack was pinned under not one, but a tangle of branches. It was going to be a slow job to free him. He was about to start, when a wolf howled on the hillside.

With the wolves on the prowl, Jack's father knew there wasn't time to cut the limbs. He must shift the tree. Bracing his feet, he grabbed a branch in his mouth and tugged with all his might. The tree didn't budge. At that moment, a bulky figure loomed out of the darkness. It was One Paw. Together, the two beavers gave the tree another mighty heave.

Jack felt the tree lift, and with seconds to spare, squirmed out from under it.

Chapter Nine

LEAVING HOME

The following spring, a few hours after the ice had gone, Jack heard the distant clamor of geese. Their wild cries stirred something deep within him. As the geese drew closer, he could make out the calls of individual birds, *Aahonnk ahonnk ahonnk!* Moments later the flock appeared over the trees at the top of the valley.

The geese were headed north, flying in vee formation. As Jack watched, the flock wavered, then changed direction. Gabbling to each other, the huge gray birds turned and began to lose altitude. On stiff wings they glided straight for the pond.

The Canada geese splashed down in the center of the pond, near the lodge. For a minute or two every head with its white cheek patch looked around, alert for danger. Then most of the geese tucked their long black necks under their wings and went to sleep. They had flown all the way from Tennessee.

That evening, when the shadows lengthened, the geese resumed their journey to Hudson Bay.

Their noisy departure made Jack feel even more restless. He was now two years old, and it was time that he too, should go. With the honking of the geese still ringing in his ears, he decided to strike out on his own that night.

One Paw followed Jack down to the entrance tunnel. Somehow the old beaver knew that the young beaver was leaving the colony. For a long moment, the two looked at each other. Then One Paw turned and limped back to his corner.

Jack climbed over the dam and set off downstream — the same stream that had swept him away as a kit. This time he walked along the shore, pausing frequently to check for danger, until he reached another beaver pond. At the upper end of the pond, Jack came upon a scent mound.

The mound was another beaver's boundary marker. It looked like a pie and was made of mud scooped from the bottom of the pond. After the beaver had completed its work, it had left a message by spraying the mound with strong smelling oil from the glands under its tail.

Jack sniffed the mound and learned that a family of beavers occupied the pond. He'd seen his father chase wandering male beavers away, and he knew he would not be welcome. So he skirted the edge of the pond and continued on his way.

Before dawn, Jack bedded down between some boulders at the edge of the stream. He stayed there until the following night, then slowly worked his way down the stream. The next pond he came to was also occupied by a colony of beavers. Once again, to avoid conflict with the father beaver, he kept on going.

He wanted to find a home of his own. He had lived in a pond all his life, so it was natural that he would look for a pond. However, by the time he reached the lake, he had passed four beaver ponds. All of them were occupied. The lake didn't seem suitable either, for it was much too big to dam.

At dusk, Jack set off to explore the shoreline of the lake. After an hour he came upon a brook that spilled into the lake. His beaver instinct told him to follow it. Turning his back on the lake, he walked inland. As he slowly ambled upstream he noticed that the creek flowed through a shallow valley, and that it was edged with alder bushes.

Suddenly the brook disappeared into a round hole under a hump of ground. Jack crossed the hump, and saw to his surprise that the water also flowed on the other side. This puzzled him, for he didn't know the hole was a culvert, and the dirt-covered hump was a road.

Retracing his steps, he started downstream, back to the lake. On the way he spied a fine place to build a dam. The spot was fairly close to the culvert but hidden behind a screen of trees. With a start he realized that, if he could dam the brook, he would have his own pond!

Before doing anything, Jack checked the lay of the land on both sides of the brook. He was pleased with what he saw. The ground was low enough that a small rise in the water level would cover it.

It was already growing light when he reached the lake. Jack bedded down under a fallen spruce tree a few steps from the lake. If danger threatened, he could quickly escape into the water. The fallen spruce would remain his den until his pond was filled to a safe depth.

•

The setting sun had touched the treetops when Jack went back up the brook. At the site he'd chosen, there were several boulders in the water. These would serve to anchor his dam. He began by cutting down the nearest alder bushes on both sides of the brook. Carefully he wedged the alders between the boulders with their butts pointing upstream. By the end of the night, a ragged line of alder bushes and boulders stretched from bank to bank. The water flowed freely through the branches, but it was a start.

The following evening he discovered that the current had washed away some of his alders. After replacing the alders, he looked around the streambed for rocks to weigh them down. It was slow work, for he could only carry one rock at a time in his forepaws. A few of the larger ones he rolled into place with his shoulder.

The next night he added another layer of alders. These too were weighted with stones. Then he scooped up armfuls of mud from the bottom. Clutching the mud to his chest, he walked on his hind legs back to the dam and packed it among the sunken branches. It took him many trips to complete the job.

Now the foundation was laid, Jack needed larger sticks and small logs to build the wall of the dam. He could have cut some of the nearby evergreens, but he didn't like the taste of their bark. Like all beavers, he preferred to use building materials that he could also eat. Jack remembered a grove of young birch trees near the mouth of the brook. The grove was on a little point that jutted into the lake.

When he visited the grove the next evening, he saw there was a cottage on the other side of the point. Quietly slipping into the water, he swam downwind of the wooden building. He caught a faint whiff of humans, but it was an old scent. To be on the safe side, he watched the cottage for more than an hour before he cut down the first birch.

The trees were small and all about the same size. It was easy to cut them into manageable sections and tow them down the lake to the mouth of the brook. From there, he dragged them up the brook to the dam. Within a week the wall of the dam was finished, and the water had flooded both banks. Jack's pond was beginning to take shape.

•

Late one afternoon a dusty station wagon stopped on the dirt road that led to the cottage. A man, his wife, their two children, and the family dog all got out of the car to stare at the sheet of water covering the road.

"What's happened?" the boy asked his father.

"I'm not sure, but it looks like the work of a beaver to me."

"Can we drive through it?" asked his eight-year-old daughter.

"I'll try, but we may get stuck," answered her father.

By going slowly so as not to create a wave, the family managed to get to the cottage. As soon as they arrived, the children ran to the lake and the dog went in for a swim. After the car was unloaded and everything unpacked, the parents took a stroll down to the lake. The mother glanced toward the point.

"Oh, my goodness! Look at our birch grove!"

"It's the beaver!" exclaimed her husband. "It's cut nearly every tree."

"What a shame. Is there anything we can do?" asked his wife.

"The first thing I'm going to do," replied her husband grimly, "is get rid of the beaver."

CHAPTER TEN

A NEW LIFE

The lake was shrouded in mist when the children tiptoed out of the cottage. Quietly they made their way through the strip of woods to the beaver pond. The previous day their father had cut a large hole in the dam. By the time he was finished, water was gushing out of the pond. The children were anxious to see what had happened to the beaver.

The pond shone like a mirror in the early morning light. The water level was just the same as before. Hiding themselves in the bushes, they waited, hoping to see the beaver. Presently he emerged from the water near the hole in the dam. He had a stick in his mouth. With great care he placed the stick on top of the dam, as the finishing touch to the repairs he had made.

The children watched, spellbound. Without

thinking, the girl slapped a mosquito on her arm.
The beaver heard the tiny sound and scuttled into the
water. He popped up on the far side of the pond,
whacked the surface with his tail, then dove again.
That was the last they saw of him.

As they were leaving, the girl turned to her
brother. "Do you think we should wake Dad and tell
him the beaver's fixed the dam?"

"No, we should let him sleep," replied her brother.
"He'll find out soon enough!"

•

A few days later, a green panel truck came to the
cottage. A man from the wildlife department stepped
out of the dripping vehicle. The children's father had
called the department for help. The officer looked
around the pond and examined the dam. Then he
went to his truck and got a live trap — a trap that
would capture the beaver so that it could be released.

The trap was the size and shape of a large suitcase.
It had an aluminum frame and wire mesh sides. The
trap was set by opening the two sides like the pages of
a book. When the trigger was touched, the spring-
loaded sides snapped together, imprisoning the
animal between the mesh.

Rather than baiting the trap, the man decided to place it so the beaver would step on it. The spot he chose was on a path at one end of the dam. The trap was laid flat in the shallows and anchored with a chain attached to a stake. Setting the trap under water not only helped to conceal it but also masked the smell of humans.

•

Resting in his den by the lake, Jack heard the man driving the stake into the ground. The sounds made him nervous. That night he approached the pond, with extra care. Instead of going around the end of the dam, as he usually did, he skirted through the undergrowth. And he didn't enter the water right away, but stayed in the bushes to look and listen. Everything seemed normal. At the end of the evening, he took his usual route to leave the pond.

Just as he stepped out of the pond, the water exploded around him. At the same instant, he was struck from both sides and flung to the ground. Jack tried to dive back into the water, but was held fast. He was trapped.

•

The man from the wildlife department came back the next morning. When he returned from checking the trap, the family was waiting for him. The man wore heavy gloves and held the trap away from his body with both hands. The beaver was at the bottom, squeezed between two layers of chain link mesh.

"I got him," said the wildlife officer.

"Do you think there are any more there?" asked the father.

"There's no lodge, and this is a young beaver. From the tracks I've seen, I'm pretty sure he's alone."

"What's going to happen to him?" asked the little girl.

"I'll release him about an hour's drive from here."

"What sort of place is it?" said the boy.

"Now, kids," the children's father broke in, "don't bother the officer with questions."

"That's okay. They're fair questions," said the officer. "I'm going to drop this beaver off beside a pond that was trapped out a couple of years ago."

The children looked at each other, then the girl asked, "What does 'trapped out' mean?"

"It means there are no beavers there — they were all caught by trappers."

"Will the beaver be all right alone?"

"He should be," grunted the man, hoisting the trap into the back of the truck. As he closed the doors, he added half to himself, "If he doesn't get caught next winter."

•

Jack lay on his side on the floor of the truck. The way the trap was placed, he couldn't see anything, nor could he move. As the vehicle hummed along, his mind went blank and he slipped into a trance.

The terror came back with a rush when the truck left the highway. It rattled over a dirt road, swaying from side. Then, slowing to a crawl, the truck bucked and twisted down a logging trail. At last it stopped.

Jack heard the man open the back door, and felt the trap move. A moment later he was blinking in the sunlight and he could smell water. The man flipped the catches on the trap. The wire mesh fell away. He was free!

Jack made a dash for the pond and plunged into the water. He stayed under until he was well out from shore. Only then did he surface to check on the human. The man was standing by the truck. The beaver slapped the water with his tail and dove again.

The next time he came up, he didn't look back, but headed straight for the opposite shore.

Jack knew that he must get away from the humans. On the far shore he found the river that fed the pond. His instinct told him to follow the river. Swimming and trotting along the bank, he worked his way upstream. At dawn the next morning, he denned for the day in a hollow log.

Driven by fear, he set off again that afternoon. As he continued up the river, he saw the countryside had changed. He was in a land of granite outcroppings, ragged jack pines, black spruce, and birch. Later that night he came upon a patch of low ground where a brook entered the river. A scent mound at the mouth of the brook told him there was an active beaver colony nearby. He continued on.

During the next few days Jack kept a steady pace and covered a lot of ground. Traveling alone, he had to be on the alert even when he was at rest. One day he was dozing under a ledge when a black bear cub strayed into his hideaway. The mother bear caught Jack's scent, and charged him. Jack barely had time to plunge into the river.

There were also wolves in the area. One night, as

he approached a cluster of boulders by the river, Jack caught the faint scent of wolf. Without hesitation, he dove into the water. As he was swept downstream, he caught a glimpse of the wolves that had been waiting in ambush. To make sure they wouldn't follow, he let the current carry him around a bend, then got out on the opposite bank.

He had only gone a little way when he came upon a large stream that flowed into the river. To escape the wolves, he left the main river and followed the stream. He kept going all night. By now his muscles were hardened by constant travel.

An hour after the sun rose, Jack crossed an invisible boundary. He had entered a national wilderness park — a vast tract of land where hunting and trapping were not allowed. A gray jay, the northern cousin of the blue jay, whistled a welcome to him, *Wheeoo, wheeoo, wheeoo.*

•

A few days later, deep in the park, Jack came upon a sheltered valley with a stream running through it. Poplars, aspens and birch trees grew in the meadows that bordered the stream. He finally had found the place he had been looking for!

He was wondering where he would build a dam, when he saw in the distance another beaver. The stranger turned out to be a female who, like Jack, had left her home earlier that summer. Her name was Dawn. From the moment they met, they were friends.

As neither beaver had a home, and they both wanted to live in this valley, they agreed to share it. During August they completed the dam. By mid-September, the pond was deep enough for a lodge. When the lodge was finished, Jack and Dawn set to work, felling trees for their winter cache.

Next spring they would start a family.